It Looked
Like Spilt Milk

by Charles G. Shaw

HARPER & ROW, PUBLISHERS
NEW YORK, EVANSTON AND LONDON

IT LOOKED LIKE SPILT MILK

Sometimes it looked
like Spilt Milk.
But it wasn't Spilt Milk.

Sometimes it looked
like a Rabbit.
But it wasn't a Rabbit.

Sometimes it looked

like a Bird.

But it wasn't a Bird.

Sometimes it looked
like a Tree.
But it wasn't a Tree.

Sometimes it looked

like an Ice Cream Cone.

But it wasn't an Ice Cream Cone.

Sometimes it looked
like a Flower.
But it wasn't a Flower.

Sometimes it looked
like a Pig.
But it wasn't a Pig.

Sometimes it looked
like a Birthday Cake.
But it wasn't a Birthday Cake.

Sometimes it looked

like a Sheep.

But it wasn't a Sheep.

Sometimes it looked
    like a Great Horned Owl.
But it wasn't a Great Horned Owl.

Sometimes it looked

like a Mitten.

But it wasn't a Mitten.

Sometimes it looked

like a Squirrel.

But it wasn't a Squirrel.

Sometimes it looked
like an Angel.
But it wasn't an Angel.

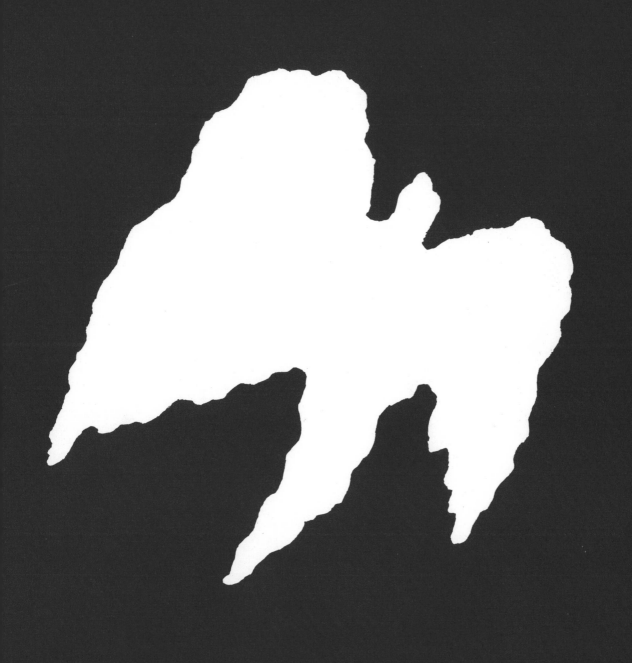

Sometimes it looked
    like Spilt Milk.
But it wasn't Spilt Milk.

It was just a Cloud in the Sky.